Cowboy

I was never a believer in love at first sight. Then I saw him. I had been used and abused so many times that I had given up on love, but looking at that cowboy standing at the end of my bar that night made me think I'd be willing to try again. He was tall and had long brown hair, just curling out from under his Stetson. All dressed in black, I couldn't see how well he filled out his jeans but when he turned to me to order a drink, his aqua blue eyes stopped me in my tracks.

"Pardon me?" I stuttered, thinking boy, what an impression I'm making.

He smiled "Can I have another beer please?"

I handed him his beer and then this famous line, "Are you new in town? I haven't seen you in here before."

He pushed back his hat a little and smiled a gorgeous white smile against an outdoor workingman's tan. "Yeah, I guess you could say I'm new." He extended his hand "Name's Travis Jordan. I'm the new foreman on the Mountain View Ranch. And you are?"

For a minute I must have looked really silly. "I, I, I'm Louanne and this is my bar." What a stupid thing to say I thought.

He grinned "Yeah, that would explain the neon 'Louannes' sign right outside."

"I'm sorry," I laughed, wondering if I looked okay in my old jeans and jean shirt, covered by a dirty white apron. "I don't know what's gotten into me tonight. It must be a full moon."

Again he smiled, "Well. This has been my first official night off so I've come to town to see what's around for excitement. Besides your bar and a movie theater, there don't look like much. So, tell me Louanne, do you ever employ another bartender or is it just you?"

"Why? Are you looking for a side job?" I smiled, glad that the knots in my tongue were loosening.

"No, the ranch keeps me busy enough. I was just wondering if you could come out from behind there long enough for a dance."

I drew back a little. This was too easy. He was probably some drifter cowboy just looking for a good time and I had had more than my share of those.

"Sorry," I heard myself saying, "but I work here most nights myself as you can see." I was popping lids and filling trays. "The orders pretty much come open to close."

He smiled sheepishly, "Well, that's too bad Louanne cause you are one pretty lady, and I think that every pretty lady should dance, especially under a moon like tonight." With that, he finished his beer, paid his tab, tipped his hat to me and walked out the door.

Sally rushed over "My Lord woman, who was that masked man?!" She joked, her southern drawl on full. "He is one handsome gentleman if I ever did see one." Sally was just what everyone expected Sally to be when they heard that lilting speech. She was an outrageous flirt, a tall, busty redhead who's hips had just enough padding to make darn good pillows as she would say. She was also

Louanne's only waitress and her very best friend.

I wiped my hands on my dirty apron and grinned at her, "His name is Travis Jordan. He's the new foreman out at the MV. He seems nice enough–"

"Nice enough hell!" she interrupted "That boy is hot, hot, hot! He just may be giving that old fart of mine something to worry about." She laughed.

"Oh Sally" I smiled "The only thing that would ever break up you and Stu is the grim reaper himself and you know it! You still light up like a Christmas tree every night when he walks into this bar" I paused to look at my watch. "Which he will be doing in about two minutes. "LAST CALL EVERYBODY!!!" I yelled over the din of the jukebox and chatter.

Then both Sally and I turned, looked at the door and like magic, Stu walked in, and, as predicted, Sally lit up. " Stu honey!" She waved "I'm over here".

As I filled the last drink orders of the night I watched Stu and Sally. They had been married for fifteen years. Every night she worked till the last call. Stu would come in to have one beer and one dance with his "Ladybug" as he called her. It was always the same song. One time when the man came to update the cd's in the juke, Sally had nearly eaten him alive when he tried to replace their song. I watched them moving on the floor, looking into each other's eyes as Patsy Cline's "Crazy" played for the millionth time on that old juke. The few stragglers, still lingering over their last beer, sang and applauded as Stu and Sally kissed at the end.

I joined in with the applause, tears welling in my eyes. How I wished I could find a love like that. With everyone gone, Stu and Sally helped me wipe the tables and set up the chairs and then they said their goodnights as well.

At the door Sally paused for a moment and put her hand to my cheek. " I know what you're thinking tonight darling and I know you've had some rough times but I guarantee you that the right man is going to find you! With that, she kissed my cheek and took Stu's arm calling, "See you tomorrow!" over her shoulder.

    I waved and turned back to the bar, closing and locking the door. I walked back behind the bar and picked up a cleaning rag, lovingly dusting the pictures of my parents that hung behind the bar. This bar had been their dream and they named it for me. I remember the love that used to shine in their eyes when they looked at each other. My father could be stern when he had to, functioning as bartender and bouncer if necessary. He had been a big handsome bear of a man and my mother was a tiny little lady. Tears well in my eyes tonight as I remembered. They had raised a good daughter. Though the bar had certainly never made them rich, they put away for my education and when the time had come, they saw to it that I went to the college of my choice. I had always loved animals and I chose a small Veterinary College about a thousand miles from home. Those thousand miles felt more like ten thousand to me, but I worked hard and went home whenever I could.

During my second semester I began working side by side with Michael Samson. I still remember the first time I saw him. He was tall and blond with mischievous green eyes. We fell in love and before I knew it, we were moving in together. Now instead of going home, I was calling home, and in the excitement of my first big romance, I somehow missed the sadness in my Mom's voice when I talked to her. One Sunday morning, after a long tender love-making session and a brunch in bed of fresh raspberries and sweet cream, the phone rang. It was Mom.

I knew as soon as I heard her voice that something was terribly wrong. "Mom? What's wrong?" I asked.

She was holding back tears as she said "It's your Father dear. It's very bad. You'd better come home as soon as possible." I didn't need to hear any more. I was running around packing my bags when I noticed Michael just standing there. "You're going? Just like that?" He said in a cruel bark that I had never heard before. "What, Mommy calls and you go running?!"

I stopped in my tracks "Michael, there's something wrong with my Father. I have to go. I want to go. What's wrong? If it's something serious I can always come back in the next semester. Why don't you come with me?"

He snickered, "Sorry, I worked damn hard to get out of a hick town like that and I'm never going back to another one!"

It now occurred to me how little Michael and I had actually talked to each other. I knew very little about his family and suddenly I had the feeling that I didn't want to know.

"Look," I said, pulling on my boots and grabbing my hastily packed bags, "I'll call you as soon as I know what's happening. We'll keep in touch and maybe I'll be back sooner than we think."

All at once he softened back to the Michael that I knew and he helped me put on my coat. He kissed me and told me that he hoped my father would be okay and then he sent me on my way.

I remember the long drive home wondering about what could possibly be wrong with my father and about Michael's strange reaction. The closer I got to Fairview, the more nervous I became and the faster I drove. I had a terrible premonition that if I weren't there soon, I would never see my father alive again. What could have happened in the six months since I'd seen him last? He had been so happy, showing me some of the new renovations they had done to the bar. I remember him twirling me around till I giggled like a little girl on the new dance floor as he said, "Country music's making a comeback little girl and people are going to dance again!"

As I pulled up to the bar, sure enough ol' Doc Peters was there. I recollect running in the bar and up the stairs to the living quarters and straight into my mother's arms. She held me for a long while and I could feel her tears on my shoulder and her body shook. "Oh Louanne," she cried "Thank God you're here."

My voice filled with emotion, "Mom, Mom, it's okay, it's okay" I patted her back. "What's wrong with Daddy?"

She sat me down at the kitchen table and took my hands into her tiny ones. "It's cancer sweetie. He doesn't have long."

The memory of those words hit me as I stood in the bar with my hand on his picture. Yes, cancer had taken my big bear of a father and it had wasted him away. He refused to be hospitalized and was hanging on by the strength of his will. He was so medicated he could barely speak coherently. He still managed to tell both his wife and his little girl how much he loved them. He vowed he would protect them from up in Heaven if he could and he went finally to his peaceful rest.

Alone in the bar, memories flowed down my cheeks and I could see my mother standing at his open coffin, promising him that she loved him and that she wouldn't be too long behind. She tried to be strong and help me keep the bar open, but without Daddy, her heart just wasn't in it. She would look longingly at the end of the bar where Daddy used to hold court with all the good ol'boys. I'd see tears in her eyes, as she would gently caress one of his old sweaters she had taken to wearing. During the afternoons she would head upstairs and lay down for a nap. One dreadful day that was where I found her. She was clutching her locket with Dad's picture in it. She had died quietly in her sleep.

I buried her next to Daddy and spent the next several days weeping and trying to decide what to do with the rest of my life. Finally, I called Michael. He had never bothered to attend either funeral. He had sent flowers, small and cheap arrangements. I called him and I told him that I thought our relationship had been reduced to small and cheap as well. By the end of our conversation I had made up my mind. Louanne's really was mine now.

Standing there gazing at their pictures I snapped back to reality. "Louanne!" I could hear my father saying, "C'mon now girl! Quit your day dreamin', there's work to be done!" And so I did. I wiped down the bar and bagged

all the garbage. I opened the back door to take it out, looked up, and saw a silvery moon.
Shaking my head I thought to myself, that must be why I'm so melancholy tonight. I stood and looked at the moon for a long time wondering about the direction my life had taken. It had been ten years since my parent's deaths. I was thirty-two now and had never been married. Oh sure, since Michael, there had been men in my life but somehow they never lasted. Either they wanted to take me away from the bar, or that was all they were interested in and not really me. Finally, I said goodnight to Mr. Moon and headed upstairs.

    I ran myself a hot bath and stood naked before the mirror, taking a good look at myself. I wasn't an ogre by any means. About 5'6' tall, I weighed a hundred and thirty pounds, most of it in the right places. Long, brown hair that streaked with gold in the summer. During the afternoons in the Summer I would help anybody who asked from gardening to ranching. Why wouldn't a man want this? I giggled to myself as I lowered my body into the hot bubbly water. The problem was Fairview. It was a small town and most of the men in it were already married or gone to the ranches and more interested in rodeos than wedding bells. I vowed to myself that if Travis Jordan were to come into my bar again, Sally could tend bar and if he didn't ask me to dance, I'd ask him! Laying my head at last on my pillow that night I looked out the window at the silver moon and as I drifted off to sleep, I thought of Travis's big blue eyes.

Early the next morning the phone awakened me. Picking up I heard the craggy old voice of Cheryl Lester, half owner of Mountain View Ranch.

"Is that you Louanne honey?" Without waiting for me to answer she continued, "Listen doll, I got a heck of a problem here! As you know it's brandin time and the darn camp cook I just hired just plumb never showed his nose! Now here I am with 40 extra hands to feed and only my own two hands to do it with! Now hon, I know it's a lot to ask, but could you come and give me a hand? I already asked Sally and she said if you was willin' she'd pick you up. What do you say?"

Wiping the sleep out of my eyes and thinking it might give me a chance to see Mr. Travis Jordan again, I quickly agreed "Sure Cheryl we'll be there as quick as we can."

I called Sally "Well c'mon" I joked "we're burnin' daylight!" She laughed and said she'd be right along.

I brushed my hair and put on an old pair of Levi's that were faded and fit just like a glove. I even had time to brush on a hint of blush so that I looked a little more awake than I was.

The drive to Mountain View was through some of the most spectacular landscape that Montana had to offer. My father had been friends with John Lester and occasionally when we had gone visiting, I had ridden through the property. Or at least as much of it as I could. The Lester family had always owned the MV and people said it would take a week to cross the property and a month to go around. Needless to say the Lesters were the wealthiest family of Fairview. They farmed part of the property for their own use but the rest was strictly cattle and in this mountainous terrain, it took a lot of cowhands to keep this ranch running.

Driving past a large stand of beautiful Aspen we came to a sign that read "Mountain View Ranch" and right below that, another sign that the area gossips had always found strange. It said, "Enter freely and leave the same." To my way of thinking it was just the opposite of a no trespassing sign but I never had the nerve to question any of the Lesters about it. I had gone to school with two of their daughters, Lisa and Carla, but as soon as they were old enough, they headed for the big city. There was a brother a few years older than me that I vaguely remembered, but rumor was that he was the black sheep of the family and his father sent him away.

    At last we arrived at the huge log home and Cheryl was coming out to meet us. We were no sooner out of the pickup when she grabbed our arms and headed us in the direction of a big tent set up in the field directly behind the house. From the tent we could hear laughter and someone playing the harmonica. " I've managed to keep them busy with coffee and biscuits so far ladies but we better get cooking on them bacon and eggs cause there is nothing worse than a bunch of hungry cowpoke!"

    Sally and I grinned at each other over the short little lady's head as she dragged us to the makeshift kitchen. She threw a couple of aprons at us and started me on the bacon and Sally on the eggs. "How do they like their eggs?" asked Sally.

"Today," she grumbled " And every day till I get me a real cook, they are likin' them scrambled!"

Sally and I worked harder at that breakfast than either of us remembered working for a long time. It amazed me that normally one cook did it all. Ten pounds of bacon and seven dozen eggs later, all the men had been fed. They had all been polite, lining up, taking off their hats, filling their plates. Each and every one of them saying thank you to Sally and I for going out of our way. There had been more than one handsome fella in the bunch, but none of them were Travis Jordan. Sally, Cheryl and I were doing clean up when we heard the sound of a galloping horse headed our way.

Without looking up, Cheryl said "That'd be Travis. He was up earlier than the others. Say one thing for the boy, he learned the value of hard work somewhere."

Suddenly, there he was, riding up to us on a large black stallion. He dismounted, handing a nearby cowboy the reins saying, "Take him to the barn and wipe him down good. He's already had a hard ride this morning." He turned to us. "Good morning ladies, I see my mother has you working up a sweat."

My mouth dropped open and Sally elbowed me as she said, "Mother? You're Travis Lester? I thought you were earning your living in the big city somewhere—"

Travis grinned. "I was, but the ranch called me home after Dad had his stroke. So till he's on his feet again I'm here to take care of things." He turned to me "Seems that something sad made us both realize where we belong. Right Louanne?" Then he turned and headed to the corral where the horses were kept, yelling "C'mon guys! Down that coffee! We got cows to brand and from my scouting expedition this morning we are gonna spend half the week just getting them all in!"

For the next couple of minutes it was like being back in time watching all those men saddle up and ride past heading out to do the job the same way they had for a hundred years. John Lester held onto the old ways and for those minutes standing there watching, I was glad he did. It was like watching history come to life.

Travis was the last to ride by. He pulled up the large Bay he was riding now into a stand like the lone ranger and tipped his hat to us. At least I thought it was to us. Sally hooted as he rode off. "Oh girl, he's got his eye on you!" She was giggling like a schoolgirl. I swatted her and she swatted me back and soon we were both giggling, with Cheryl looking at us like we'd gone off our rockers.

Finally, I managed to catch my breath long enough to ask, "Cheryl, last night Travis introduced himself to me and I'm sure he called himself Travis Jordan!?"

Cheryl grunted "Yeah, that's his middle name. Since him and his Daddy had that falling out years ago he's gone by that. It's not legal though. That boy is Travis Jordan Lester whether he wants to be or not."

Sally piped up "How is John? Is he walking yet?? Any idea when you might expect him home?" Mr. Lester was currently in a rehabilitation hospital.

Cheryl sighed, " He's not doing as well as we had hoped. Seems like his heart isn't in it. What do you expect when you work hard all your life to give your children a good home, and then they grow up and they turn their backs on you?" We were quiet. It seemed like the grizzled old lady had something to get off her chest.

"Lisa and Carla have visited him once! Once in eight darn months! And Travis?! Well Travis won't visit his Daddy at all, but at least John knows that he's here and he's running the ranch for him. I wanted to hire a private nurse and bring him home but Travis says that if he has to put up with him telling him how to run things he won't do it. So what do you do? Ladies there's no tellin' when you hold a baby in your arms what that child's gonna turn out like!" There were tears in her eyes.

I couldn't help myself. I reached out and hugged her. She froze for a second in my arms but I didn't let go and then I could feel like her heart was breaking. This poor tough old lady was trying her best to keep things together and it seemed like she wasn't getting much support. All of a sudden Travis didn't look so good to me. No matter what they had fought over I thought he should visit his father now before it was too late.

Cheryl pulled away, embarrassed. She wiped her eyes. "Look at me.", forcing a smile, "A silly old woman crying over things that's in God's hands. Louanne, Sally, thank you for coming out to help me this morning. I couldn't have done it without you." She reached into her pocket and pulled out two one-hundred-dollar bills "Here, I want you to have this for helping." She said, trying to hand us the money. "Now, go on. You take it please!"

Sally and I both backed away and just headed for the truck. "Cheryl," I said, over my shoulder, "we were just being neighborly and you don't need to pay us." We got in the truck and I rolled my window down as she came up to the side.

"Louanne," she started "I remember when your Daddy used to bring you up here to ride and you loved it. Now you just bring yourselves up here anytime you want and Billy will saddle you any horse you want to ride. You're both welcome here anytime."

As we drove back to town we sat in silence until Sally said, "That's one sad family isn't it? All that money—just goes to show that money don't mean everything. Ever since Travis wrecked that car ___"

I didn't know what she was talking about. "Huh? What car? Do you know what the falling out with his Dad was over?"

"Oh yeah," said Sally, taking a second to light a cigarette. "That was all the talk of the town in those days. I think you were away at school and then when you came back you had your own share of troubles so you probably just never heard the rumors. Seems on his twenty-first birthday, John gave Travis a Porsche. Can you imagine? I never thought John Lester could part with that much money for a gift but he did. Travis had it exactly one week before he got drunk and totaled it against a tree on a road to the ranch. Now Travis was hurt too, hurt bad.

For a while they didn't think he'd make it. He was in a coma for a month or more; he broke both legs and most ribs. He had some brain swelling, you know, how they talk about concussions these days? Well, we didn't know that then." She shrugged "When he woke up he had to relearn everything, I mean everything! Reading, writing, walking, even speech and what did John Lester do? That boy was barely on his feet when Mr. Lester lets him have it with a full head of steam he'd been saving up about wrecking that stupid car. A friend of mine was a nurse at the hospital and she said that he went on at Travis so bad and so long that when he was done Travis had to be sedated, which was very dangerous seeing as he had been in a coma. Imagine, Sheila, my nurse friend said that everyone that overheard got the impression that the darn car was more important to John than Travis. Well, as soon as Travis was released from the hospital, he left. Took the Greyhound out of town and from then till the other night in the bar was the first time he's been back. I didn't even recognize him. Takes after his father though now that I think about it. John Lester was the cock of the walk at one time."

I sat quietly thinking that maybe Travis did have reason to bear a grudge against his father after all. "Well, someone must have known where he was, otherwise how would he know to come home?"

Sally stubbed out her cigarette. "I think he wrote to his mama every so often, Louanne. To tell the truth, I really don't know. But I do know he was checking you out this morning!" She laughed, "You'd better be prepared cause the day they are finished branding all them cowboys are going to hit the bar and Travis Jordan Lester will be looking for you!"

I said " Oh Sally don't be silly." But I was hoping she was right.

So, for the next ten days life went on as normal. I opened my bar at four as always and I closed at one as always. Stu and Sally danced every night and every night I imagined it was Travis and I holding each other and looking into each other's eyes the way they did. I had to face it, I was falling in love with a man I hardly knew. But I somehow knew we both had loneliness in our hearts and that maybe we could heal each other. Sally had heard that Cheryl had indeed found herself a camp cook so she hadn't needed any more help from us. Every day I listened for rumors of the MV, how branding was going, and had the cowhands seen any of Montana's vanishing grizzlies. Then one day, one of the cowhands wandered in and asked for me. Sally directed him to the bar.

He politely took off his hat as he approached me. "Are you Miss Louanne?" he grinned sheepishly.

Lord, how I love these cowboys' manners I thought to myself. They just know how to make a woman feel like a lady. "Yes, I am." I answered, "What can I do for you?"

"Well Ma'am, Mrs. Lester sent me down here to warn you that we'd be done branding tomorrow and it was only fair that we should warn you. So, you know, you might want to hire to have extra help and all." He was grinning from ear to ear.

I had to grin to myself. "Just how many of you should I expect tomorrow night?"

He looked surprised. "Why---all of us I expect!" With that he nodded, put his hat back on and left.

Sally came rushing over. "What was that all about?" I told her and she said "What? Those cowboys come in here every year after branding and after every other dang thing they do up there and that's the first time you ever got a warning they were coming. That's Cheryl: She's got matchmaking on her mind! Ahuh! She saw the way Travis looked at you and she wants him to stay and she likes you so put two and two together!" Sally crowed triumphantly. I nearly doubled over from laughing. "Sally, I hate to disappoint you, but I'm sure Cheryl just thinks she's returning a favor like we did for her the other day."

"Oh yeah? Then why make such a big production of it? Hasn't she heard of the phone? She did the other day? No way Louanne, Cheryl is daughter in law hunting. You mark my words!"

The rest of the day was uneventful with the exception of Ally demanding to take over the bar while I went shopping to get myself something new to wear the next night. "Get something green.", she had said. Something green to bring out the green in my eyes. "And lipstick!" She had yelled at my back, "Don't forget lipstick!" So I found myself in Fairview's one small mall, shopping for clothes, which I hadn't done in ages. It wasn't that I couldn't afford it. The bar had been paid off long before my parents had died. It netted me a tidy profit every month and, except for groceries and household bills, the rest went into the bank. After ten years I had become a lady of means and I suppose I could have retired somewhere warm. But Fairview was my home and the bar had become my life. I bought myself several new pairs of jeans, pleased to find out I still fit a size 8 and then I spied a beautiful emerald green sweater. It was cashmere and an extravagant price, but I fell in love with the way it felt against my skin and hugged my curves. Armed with bags and packages, I headed to the cosmetics counter and was surprised to see free makeovers for purchasing a certain perfume. It happened to be a scent I loved, so I bought it and asked for the makeover. The cosmetician was a girl I had gone to school with, Heather, and while she did my makeover we caught up on old times and she showed me pictures of her baby. Finally she said "There, you're done!" and when I looked into the mirror I barely recognized myself. She had kept it natural looking as I had asked her, but my skin glowed, my green eyes stood out like green pools of mountain water. My lips looked like they were waiting to be kissed and I hoped in my heart the next night they would be.

When I walked back into the bar and up to Sally her mouth fell open. "Girl, you are beautiful! You went whole hog!" I told her about the free makeover. "Do you remember how to do it?" She asked " You are gonna have everyone of those cowboys panting over you tomorrow night, never mind Travis Lester."

The rest of the evening was spent making calls. I had decided to hire a band for the evening and make a big deal out of it. We hired a popular local band in the area. We put the news on the local media page, calling it the Harvest Dance. I called Heather and asked her if she might be interested in making some extra money, and if she had any friends who might be interested? She did. Stu watched the bar while Sally and I went for some decorations and hay bales. Feeling we had done as much as we could to make the evening a success, Sally and I headed back to the bar.

The next day I opened the bar two hours early to let the band in to set up. They were a young group that played covers of their favorite country songs. Once they were settled in and setting up, I locked the doors again and went upstairs to get myself ready. I washed my hair, I applied the make up I had purchased, exactly how I remembered Heather showing me, and I put on a new pair of jeans, a braided leather belt and tucked in that clingy, emerald green cashmere sweater. When I stood in front of my mother's old cheval mirror even I had to put modesty aside and say that I looked good. My hair gleamed and the sweater did bring out the color of my eyes, which were glowing with expectation. Expectations that I hoped weren't too high.

At three-thirty I went back down to the bar. The boys were done setting up, and asked if they could have a beer. I said sure but in the same breath, warned them to stay sober to play. Fairview hadn't seen a "do" like this since Stu and Sally had a bonfire party for their house-warming five years ago. Looking out the doors as I was opening them, I wasn't disappointed. Already there were more than the regulars waiting to come in.

I threw open the doors and yelled " Alright! It's party time people!" I felt a little silly and happy at the same time.

Stu and Sally were the first ones in. Stu had volunteered to help me tend the bar and Heather and her friend were expected at six. Well, by five pm Sally and I were already hustling our behinds just keeping the regulars and other folks that were blending together happy and there was no sign of the crew for the Mountain View Ranch yet. Heather and her giggling friend Michelle arrived right on time, a good thing; cause already the bar was more than half full. Sally and I were wondering if we shouldn't have more temporary help. At about seven-thirty Sally looked at me and said "Honey, them boys are going to pull up here any second and you might want to freshen up cause, I know I sure do!"

"Sally" I laughed "You're married!"

"Yeah, that's right" she grinned, " Married—not dead. Stu knows I'm a big flirt and that's all. I think he gets a kick out of it."

So we left Heather and Michelle to deal with the crowd, while we took a little break. We went upstairs and freshened up and then we sat at my kitchen table and each of us had a frosty beer. It tasted like liquid silk after all the work we had done. I was beginning to think that the branding was taking an extra day and while this shindig was going to make me a little more profit than usual, I had really done it to impress Travis.

Sally saw the worried look on my face "Don't you worry girl! You have a short memory or an over excited one I swear! Those boys always arrive late and stay late. Right now I have no doubt Cheryl is handing them out their pay after having stuffed them with the 'End Of Branding' steak feed like she does every year. This morning Stu saw one of those MV pickups going up the hill with a load of beer. Now those boys have had their feed, they're gonna sit around a fire, talk some, drink some, smoke some and then they will be down here, hell bent for leather by about nine."

"And just how would you know all that?" I asked. I'd known Sally for a very long time and I'd never seen her with anyone but Stu.

"Honey," She smiled. "Fifteen, almost sixteen years ago on a night very much like tonight, I met Stu in this very bar after he finished a branding at Mountain View." She laughed at the look of surprise on my face. "Stu only started up the hardware store cause of me. I didn't want a travelin' cowboy. I wanted a stay-at-home one. So Stu made the rounds a couple more years, we saved every penny and then he bought old Lawson's Hardware."

I was ogling Sally like she was a creature from another planet. "All these years I've known you and you never told me that. I just thought Stu worked at the hardware store! Why is it still called Lawson's?"

Sally drained her beer. "Cause Stu thinks having his name hung out there would make people treat him differently. You know, like he was a big shot or something. No one does that to you! Cause hell, this bar has always been 'Louannes'. I think he should change it too but after all this time, he won't, so we just don't argue about it anymore. Let me warn you of one thing Louanne, if you get mixed up with

Travis, or any cowboy, they are a breed apart and most of the breed is stubborn as hell!"

I looked at my watch and saw the time was coming up on nine. "Well, let's go down and see how right you are Mrs. Cowboy!" I teased. We walked into the bar, arms linked and giggling like we had had more than one beer at my table. The place was packed and the cowboys still hadn't arrived.

Stu waved us over to the bar "Louanne!" He grinned. "You are makin' a killing tonight my dear! I can hardly keep up with these people!" He was shouting over the band who was playing great. The dance floor was hopping. Suddenly we heard the roar of engines outside and the shouts of "Ye Haw Boys! Let's party!" And in came the MV Cowboys.

They were dressed in their Sunday best. I had never seen so many black and white Stetsons at once. They swooped down on the three remaining tables, pulled them together and sat down. I could tell they weren't drunk but they had a couple of beers under their belts already.

When Michelle and Heather approached them, their hats came off in unison. I shook my head to make sure I had seen that right. I decided I'd better step back behind the bar to help Stu with what we could tell was going to be a big order. Sure enough, Heather and Michelle, giggling away, came up to the bar.

Heather said, "They want to know if they can run a tab and they'll pay at the end of the evening." I nodded. This was common practice. "In that case," she continued, " I'll have 3 dozen beers and 7 whisky shots." Then Michelle chimed in, "And I need 2 dozen beers and 15 rum and cokes."

Stu and I gaped at each other. "You do the beer Stu, and I'll do the drinks."

I was so busy mixing drinks that I didn't even notice Travis walk up to the side of the bar. He stood there watching. Stu and I just kept twisting those caps and reloading Michelle's tray at least a dozen times. Finally we were finished with their first order.

"Wow" I said to Stu. "They are going to keep us busy all by themselves!" I noticed that Stu was not looking at me but rather, behind me. He nodded his head, "Evening Travis. Nice to see you back in town."

I whirled around so quickly that my foot slipped on a puddle of drink and down on my butt I went. Stu was making his way to help me up but Travis vaulted the bar and beat him to it.

He knelt down beside me. "Are you okay?"

I could feel my face turning crimson. "Yes, the only thing I hurt is my pride."

He smiled and took my hand to help me up. When his hand touched mine it was as if someone touched me with a live wire. I could feel myself heating up from the bottom of my toes to the top of my head.

On my feet again, I smiled, "Thank you Travis."

He didn't let go of my hand. "The last time I was here I asked you to dance but there was no one to tend the bar. Will you dance with me now?"

Stu, behind us, heard every word and was grinning from ear to ear. "Go ahead Louanne-git and have some fun. If I get a rush Sally can help me. Now git!" He growled.

    As we walked out from behind the bar, I noticed how great he looked in faded blue jeans and a plaid flannel shirt. The band was playing a waltz and when he took me in his arms I felt as though I belonged there. As we danced, we held each other close and resting my head against the warmth of his flannel shirt, I could feel his heart beating. Mine seemed to be going a mile a minute, but his, was calm. When the music ended, everyone clapped and the boys at the big table hooted. "Way to go Travis!"

    I looked up at his aqua blue eyes. "What is that all about?"

Now it was his turn to blush "Nothing." He grinned "Don't pay any attention to those fools. You look beautiful tonight Louanne. Could we dance again or is your dance card full?"

We were taking turns blushing it seemed. "Travis, even if I had a dance card, and if it were full, I think I could make another spot for you."

He smiled and picked up my hand and kissed it. "Till later then. Right now I think I should have a beer with the boys."

We backed away from one another but yet, kept looking at each other. Quite a sight in the bar I suppose. Finally, one of the cowboys shouted, "C'mon Travis, you are in love!!"

Travis didn't acknowledge the statement. He sat down and I went back behind the bar.

Sally was at my elbow in a flash "Girl, that boy has got it bad for you!" Then she caught a look of my dreamy eyes. "Hot Damn." She laughed. "Stu, I think our nights of closing the bar dancing solo are going to be over right quick!"

Stu didn't seem to agree. "Now Sally, it might not be good advice for you to be tellin' Louanne to get all crazy over Travis Lester. He was in the hardware store the other day and he made it quite clear to his Mama in front of me that once his Daddy gets well he's leavin'. So, best that Louanne don't get tied up with him.

Sally turned on him, "What's wrong with you, you old fart? Louanne can sell this place and go with him if that were the case or maybe, just maybe, he might love her enough to stay? Damn Stu, the girl needs some love in her life. Don't you go digging holes where there don't need to be none."

I butted in. "Hey, hey, calm down over here. All I did was dance with a man and you two throw a panic switch. I am well aware of just who Mr. Travis Jordan Lester is and I'm a big girl. So, if I fall head over heels in love and then land on my butt—it's my butt! Okay? Okay, case closed. Besides, here comes Heather and Michelle again and we're in for another long rush."

Long was not the proper word. For the next hour all three of us were kept busy filling orders and ringing in tabs. The cowboys' table was already sitting at well over three hundred dollars. My feet were beginning to ache but even so, I was glad to see so many people having so much fun at Louanne's. My father was probably tickled pink right now, somewhere watching over this whole thing. So far, it had been a great night. No fights, not even so much as an argument and it was going on midnight now. I had made arrangements for the band to play till two. Tonight for the first time in Louanne's history that I knew of, last call would be at two-thirty and not twelve-thirty.

Occasionally I would glance over at Travis and see him smiling and talking. It was like he could feel me looking at him, because he would look at me and smile. I was beginning to think he had changed his mind about the dance, when he finally approached.

"C'mon" he grinned, holding out his hand. "I asked the band to play a special song."

As he led me out to the dance floor and took me in his arms, the cowboys hooted and applauded loudly. The band began to play an old Eagles tune, "Desperado".

He held me even closer this time and I felt like I was floating on air. He whispered in my ear. "I'm that desperado Louanne but when I laid eyes on you the other day, I decided it was time to stop running. It's time to mend my fences and settle down. I'd like to get to know you better. How do you feel about that?"

For a moment I was stunned, but as the song ended, I whispered back that that would be just fine with me.

He walked me back to the bar and asked Stu for two beers. "Can you do without this lady for a few more minutes?" he asked Stu.

Stu nodded and before I could protest, Travis handed me a beer and led me outside. Once there, he took off his hat and looked for a moment like he was searching for something to say. Finally he said "Louanne, I remember you from when your daddy used to bring you to the ranch to ride. I don't know if you remember, but I was the one who always brought you your horse. I was pretty sullen, never said much so you might not remember."

I did remember though. I hadn't thought about it in years. I said, "I had a crush on you. I thought you might be the loneliest boy in the world and I wanted to take you home with me. But Daddy said that he didn't think your daddy would let you go." I smiled at the memory.

Travis's eyes clouded for a minute and he took a drink of his beer. "Well, my father and I don't see eye to eye on anything. We never have. I wasn't the son he wanted. The son he wanted died." He said this without bitterness, just sadness.

I was confused "You had a brother?"

Travis nodded " Yep, his name was Sam and he was everything to my Dad. He was the cowboy Dad wanted. I was more content to read. Sam was nine and I was seven when Sam fell down a well and drowned before anyone could get to him. My father believes that I left the well uncovered after getting water and so it was my fault that Sam was dead. Truth was, it was Ma who left the well uncovered but I never said anything. I'm sure she knows the truth and deals with her own guilt. Why should any of us be feeling this way after all these damn years?! No matter who left the well open, Sam died. Can't bring him back with blame!"

I sat in stunned silence. After Sally's story about the car—well the car must have just been an excuse for John Lester. "We, I mean, I thought you two were fighting over a car!?"

Travis laughed "Oh, the Porsche. Yeah, well that was what my Dad needed me to do so he could tell me just what he thought of me. I think sometimes he bought the car for that reason—he knew—hell. I was young and full of guilt and pain I didn't deserve and drinking way too much. He knew all that. Now tell me, would you give your drunk son a vehicle, never mind a Porsche?"

I shook my head, "No". "Of course you wouldn't. But John Lester handed me those keys to that new car and said, "Go get drunk son and carouse the town! You're a man now!"

I couldn't believe my ears. "Oh Travis, I'm so sorry." I had tears running down my cheeks. He turned and saw me crying and hugged me fiercely and kissed each tear.

"Don't feel sorry for me Louanne." He took my chin in his hand and raised my eyes to meet his. "I'm not looking for sympathy. My messed up family is not your problem and I don't want you to fall in love with me based on some sob story. I went on to get better, move away and make something out of myself. I left a flourishing law practice to come back here. I couldn't understand why I was still drawn here till I walked in and saw you that day. Little Louanne Reeves, all grown up—you see you weren't the only one with a crush. I just don't think I ever got over mine."

With that, he was kissing me and I was kissing him back. His lips moved down my neck to my shoulder. I felt like I was on fire and that I had better put it out before it burned too hot to stop. As much as I desired this man, I was not sleeping with him tonight.

I sighed and stepped away, taking his hand. "Let's not go too fast there cowboy." I smiled.

He laughed. "Yeah, you're right. Speed has always got me into trouble in the past, so we'll take it slow. But Louanne, I want you to know that my intentions are for the best. I'm not looking to get hurt and I'll do my very best not to hurt you okay?"

I nodded up at him, my heart feeling light in my chest. "On that, you have a deal."

Hand in hand, we walked back into the bar and I went to help Stu and Sally who were swamped. Travis went back to his table of cowboys. Later in the evening, getting close to closing, I asked the band to play "Crazy" for Sally and Stu. And as usual, as soon as the 'Last Call' for the evening rang out, Stu and Sally took the floor. Other couples were dancing and when the first strains of Crazy started they sat down. It was as if the whole town knew about this tradition of Stu and Sally's. When the song ended the whole bar applauded and Stu and Sally blushed and bowed. Why not, I thought. How often do you see a couple still so in love after so many years. People were paying their tabs and leaving while others were still lingering over that last beer.

Travis came up to me once more. "Well," he said, "since I've only had a couple, I've been elected designated driver for tonight so I've got to get these boys up the hill for the night. Most of them will be off to other ranches tomorrow, taking their horrendous hangovers with them." He reached for his wallet. "What's the tab?"

I added it up twice cause I couldn't believe it. "Travis, I'm almost embarrassed to say this but it's $742.00!"

Travis laughed. "Don't be embarrassed! I knew these boys could drink when I brought 'em here." He handed me three five-hundred-dollar bills. "See that Michelle, Heather, Sally and Stu get a tip out of that would you? You've all been real good to us tonight."

As I nodded in agreement and reached for the money, his hand closed over mine. "Can I call you in a couple of days? There's a place I'd like you to see." Again I nodded and he reached across the bar and kissed my cheek. "I gotta get. I got Roger to drive a rented party van down, but he came into the party, so I've gotta drive it back. Goodnight, my sweet Louanne."

With that he turned and hollered, " Let's go boys!!"

The cowboys dutifully followed Travis out the doors. Some staggering, but most not. They had been polite and well mannered all night. I was not surprised. All the years that the hands from the ranches in the area had been coming to Louanne's I could only remember a couple of fights breaking out and those that were involved were usually easily pacified and apologetic. As Stu, Sally, Michelle and Heather and I cleaned the bar, my thoughts were of Travis. All these years carrying around that terrible guilt over his brother's death for no good reason. What a terrible father John Lester was! But then I reminded myself to reserve my judgment until I knew Travis better. After all, every story has two sides. That was a saying that my father had quoted often and he tried to live by it. Perhaps that's why my father died a loved and respected man. It was nearly four when I ushered all my help out the door, admonishing them that they had already done more than enough. Michelle and Heather were well pleased with the extra money and the generous tip I threw in on top of the one Travis had left. Stu and Sally said they would see me the next evening as usual.

In the quiet of the empty bar, I found that I was still not tired. Too much excitement and too many late nights. I smiled. My father trained me well. I was so used to lack of sleep and strange hours that doing this or late night disc jockey was probably the only work I'd ever be suited for. I turned on the jukebox and danced my way through the last of my chores. I emptied the till and counted the night's earnings. Seeing more than a healthy total, I laughed. 'I'll be smiling all the way to the safe.' was the silly thought that passed my mind. Giggling to myself at my own silliness, I put the money in the safe, slammed it shut and whirled the dial. Walking through the bar I took one last look around before hitting the lights. I had danced with the man I would spend the rest of my life with tonight. Somehow in my heart I knew this. With a light step and a floating heart, I turned out the lights and headed off to bed.

The next few days passed uneventfully. Each day I hoped to hear from Travis and each day Sally assured me a hundred times or more that I would. But each day passed without a call. Four days after the Harvest dance I had begun to think that he had changed his mind or maybe he had just been handing me a line. I decided to give him a piece of my mind the next time I saw him, if I ever did, when he walked into the bar. From head to toe he was dirty. The only white anywhere was the whites of his eyes as he looked into mine from the other side of the bar.

"I'm so sorry Louanne!" He spoke slowly as if the words were an effort. "I came as soon as I could. You would not believe the couple of days I've had."

I grinned "Yeah, from the look of you I think I would. Would you like a beer?"

His smile was a beam of light. "That would be wonderful—I'm glad you're not angry. I'm sure you expected to hear from me by now." He accepted the beer I gave him, drained it, drinking like a parched man. "I've been in the high country chasing this one damn crazy bull." He laughed. "I've forgotten how to track properly I guess, cause this bull had me going in circles for a day and a half!"

I burst out laughing. "Oh Travis! You're lying."

He looked me right in the eye. "No." He suddenly wasn't smiling; he was very serious. "That's the one thing I never do Louanne, ever."

I hadn't meant to offend him but I knew I had. "I'm sorry Travis, I was only joking."

Now it was he who lowered his eyes. "No, I'm sorry. I'm as tired as I ever remember being and that's no excuse to snap at you. Look, I'm going to head home. I just wanted you to know that I hadn't forgotten about you. It may be a few more days but as soon as I locate and probably KILL that damn bull, I'll have some free time and," he continued, taking my hand, "I'm looking forward to spending it with you."

I smiled and he kissed my cheek and put on his hat and left. I followed him to the door and again, even as weary as he was, he pulled his horse up 'Silver style' and waved his hat at me. "I'm crazy about you Louanne Reeves. I'll see you soon." And he was gone.

I floated back to the bar. Sally was giggling at me. "I told you so." She wagged her finger. "Why, he practically proposed to you in front of half the town!"

I shook my head " I think you're watching far too many soaps Sally."

She laughed. "Soaps? My dear girl I live in a soap—have I told you about the latest gossip?" She proceeded to tell me about her sister's trouble in Abilene and how she'd taken back her drunk husband for the 20th time. I listened as well as I could but my head was crowded with thoughts of Travis. Life went on as normal for the next couple of days. I tended my bar as usual with no notable changes except maybe I smiled more than usual.

It was a stormy Thursday afternoon and I was standing in the doorway watching the thunderclouds sweep across the misty mountaintops in the distance. A Jeep came roaring down the road at a dangerous speed. I sensed that something was awfully wrong somewhere and my heart almost stopped when the jeep careened to a halt in front of the bar. Cheryl Lester almost tumbled into a mud puddle in her haste to get out of the passenger side.

"Louanne!" She ran over to where I was standing. "Can you close the bar?" She demanded.

I knew she was upset over something. I put my hands on her trembling shoulders. "What's wrong Cheryl?" What's happened?!"

Her next words filled my heart with fear. "It's Travis. He was attacked by a damn grizz up in the highlands!! We all thought he was still chasing that crazy bull." She burst into tears, "My God he laid up there, bleeding..", she sobbed, trying to form her words. "We never knew anything was wrong till his horse came back with no rider." I helped her to the bench that sat outside the bar, where she collapsed. "Even then it took us a while to find him. My God Louanne, what if I lose him too?" With those words, the damn broke and tears she had probably been holding in for years came pouring out. I put my arms around her, held her and stroked her hair. She regained her composure quickly. "C'mon, please if you can come with me."

She didn't even have to say anything. I grabbed my coat and asked Sally if she could usher out the few customers we had and close up. She had overheard much of the conversation and quickly agreed. "You go to him Honey, I'll be praying for him." She looked at Cheryl. "Stay strong Cheryl. All our thoughts are with you."

In the Jeep with Cheryl was a cowboy I hadn't seen before. Cheryl introduced him. "Louanne, this is Mike Henry. He's our pilot when we need one. Have you ever been in a small plane before? With the storm it might be a rough ride. He's in the hospital in Bankshead. Funny enough, the same one as his Dad. He keeps asking for you when he's conscious. Apparently, he fades in and out."

I didn't care if I had to ride through hell; I was going to where Travis was. "No, I haven't Cheryl but don't worry about me. Let's just get there!"

Mike Henry thought he was a pilot on land as well as in the air because we practically flew through the mountainous terrain back to the MV. The small airstrip was carved out of a field on the ranch. As I looked at the size of it I wondered how we'd even manage a take off. The fear in my mind was fear for Travis. I couldn't bear the thought of finally finding a man I knew I could love forever and then maybe losing him before we really even had a chance to begin.

The conversation was minimal as we piled into the plane. Cheryl took the back seat with me in the front with the pilot.

"Make sure your seat belts are tight." Grimaced Mike as he tightened his. "This is gonna be a rough ride. Cheryl, I wish you would just agree to drive." He muttered.

"Mike, I asked for odds, you gave me fifty-fifty." Barked Cheryl "We need to get there in a hurry. Now let's FLY.

I shook my head; our odds of getting there were fifty-fifty? Oh, it must be really bad if Cheryl is this desperate to get there.

"How did Travis get to the hospital?" I asked, hoping that he had made it in before the storm front moved in.

"He was life-flighted, only thing that could land up there was a helicopter that the ranger services use, but there wasn't enough room for me." Cheryl explained having regained some of her composure. "He was hollerin' your name over and over again as they put him in the chopper and I knew that he wanted you there.

Don't be scared Louanne," she comforted "I've flown with Mike through worse storms than this."

Mike turned and gave her a funny look and I knew she was lying, but I also understood. The last thing she needed right now was a panicked passenger. I drew my seat belt as tight as I could and hoped that the hour and a half flight to Bankshead would only take half the time.

As we took off, we were buffeted around by the wind like we were a kite. Mike had a white-knuckle grip on the wheel. Except for Mike, who once in a while uttered a curse word or two, the ride was a silent one. Silent, and sometimes, terrifying. Twice, the turbulence was so bad, the little plane groaned and rattled and once a lightning strike was uncomfortably close. After about thirty minutes we began to approach the outskirts of the storm front and blue sky could be seen in patches amongst the clouds. A few minutes later when we began our approach to the small Bankshead we were in clear sky. I never remembered being so grateful to see the sun. I hoped that our having made it through the storm was a hopeful sign that Travis would be all right. My head was filled with visions of his beautiful tanned face, pale and bloody, his aqua blue eyes filled with pain. I was jarred from my thoughts by the plane landing with a resounding thump. I looked at Mike, and he looked a good deal calmer than he had throughout our trip. "Good job Mike!" I said.

Cheryl was looking out the window "There's the limo I called for us. C'mon Henry, move this hunk of junk." She was back to her craggy old self. " I gotta boy to take care of."

"I'm moving as fast as I can Mrs. Lester." Mike shook his head, clearly thinking she should be grateful to be there alive.

Inside the limo was a fully stocked bar. Cheryl wasted no time pouring us a healthy snifter of brandy saying, " I don't know about you all but I need this." She downed hers and smiled at Mike. "C'mon don't be shy! Drink up! A couple of times on that plane I almost wet my pants."

Mike and I looked at each other and then at her and we all burst into laughter, filled with nerves and relief to be on the ground again. What lay before us was unknown at this point but that small light hearted moment buoyed all our spirits. The driver was already aware of our destination, wasted no time with small talk, and within minutes we were at the hospital.

Once inside, we were informed that Travis was in dire straits, with severe lacerations to his back, chest, stomach and legs. He was about to be rushed into surgery and was conscious, but was refusing to go until he saw someone by the name of Louanne. I couldn't believe my ears. Mike took a seat in the waiting room as Cheryl and I rushed down a long hall to where Travis lay in Emergency. A very concerned looking man approached us. "I'm Dr. Bates. Are either of you Louanne?"

With a lump in my throat, I barely managed to say, "I am."

The Dr. took my arm and led me along with Cheryl right behind. "He's a crazy man---won't go to surgery till he sees you so let's get this done. He's in rough shape so be prepared.."

Cheryl stopped at the door. "You go now." She said, "It's you he needs. Be strong, girl! No tears." she cautioned.

The white room was a stark contrast to the bloodied bandages covering Travis almost like a mummy. His dark hair surrounding his face, so pale that those aqua eyes stood out like beacons when he opened them and saw me there.

He tried to raise his hand to mine on the rail of the bed and groaned with the effort. "Louanne, you're here"

"Shh---Shh. What are you doing you crazy fool, refusing surgery?" I motioned for the orderlies waiting at the ready to start taking him out. "You're going right now and I don't want any arguments. This is no way to start a relationship Travis Jordan Lester."

I walked beside him as they wheeled him down the hall, holding the rail and wishing it was his hand but I was afraid I'd hurt him. Suddenly my tall, strong cowboy looked very young and very small. Again he opened his eyes, fighting the dark that wanted to take him and he looked at me. "Kiss me, Louanne, please kiss me," he managed to say, as the orderlies began to load him onto the elevator.

I leaned over the bed and kissed him gently. "I'll be with you Travis. You fight for me now." I whispered, "Don't leave me when I'm falling in love."

A tiny smile formed on his face and then unconsciousness took him again. I backed away and allowed the orderlies to take him the rest of the way alone. As I watched the elevator doors close, I wondered whether I'd ever see him alive again. I stood there for a minute looking at those closed doors and knowing that if he didn't survive, the doors to my heart would close as well. Then I felt a small hand on my shoulder. It was his mother. " I know what you're thinking girl and don't even let it enter your mind. That boy is a Lester through and through and he'll be back on his feet in no time. Why, he was way worse off after his car accident." At the mention of the accident a shadow passed across her face, but she continued. "Would you like to meet his father? I haven't told him about his boy yet and right now I don't intend to, but a pretty face will cheer him up."

I wondered how she expected me to keep my worry from showing but I was quickly learning that Cheryl Lester prized backbone in people more than any other quality. Still though, I was unsure. "I don't think that would be a good idea right now Cheryl. I'm sure he'd take one look at me and know that something was wrong."

She linked her arm in mine and began to practically drag me along. "Nonsense girl, you just paste a smile on that face and think happy thoughts. Think about how you and Travis will raise my grandchildren on the ranch. It will be his you know when his pa and I pass on."

I looked at this small woman with a mixture of amazement and disbelief. I didn't know whether she possessed the strength of character I thought or perhaps a touch of insanity. Travis and I hadn't even had an official date and she was at the grandchildren point already. Her son was in an operating room fighting for his life and she was telling me to paste on a smile and keep a secret. Perhaps it went back to the pioneer survival instinct. Cheryl would have fit in perfectly. She was undaunted by life's surprises, not weakened, for anything more than a moment by any event that fate threw at her. Having a backbone of steel must get uncomfortable at times, I thought to myself, and a smile couldn't help but cross my lips.

"Okay Cheryl, I'll do my best but if I feel my resolve start to fail me, I'll leave the room okay? How do you explain my being here and just who I am?"

She stopped and looked at me as though I had rocks for brains. "Your Sam Reeves daughter ain't you?! Damn girl, your daddy and John were friends for years! Just say you were in town on business and you thought you would pay your respects. Lord, why must I think of everything?" She muttered to herself. I again began to think that maybe the strain of a sick husband, injured son and a large ranch to run was having its toll on her.

    Entering John Lester's room was like a walk back into time. Apparently he had been there quite awhile and a few western things had been brought in to make him feel more at home. A beautiful quilt lay across the bed, a dream catcher of the finest quality hung in the open window moving gently in the post storm breeze and an old wooden rocker sat in one corner with a worn looking cowboy hat hanging on one of the arms. I was surprised to see that John Lester, despite his illness, was still a formidable looking man. His white hair groomed perfectly each morning with his one remaining good arm. They needn't have worried about hiding anything from him cause he was wide-awake. The nurse had already informed him that his son was in the hospital. Upon hearing this, Cheryl gave the nurse a withering look and handed John the pad of paper he now used to communicate. She held it for him while he wrote out the word "Travis?" and underlined it several times.

I watched as Cheryl touched his cheek. "I don't know yet, John. He's in bad shape."

John moaned and wrote frantically "Must talk to him, must say I'm sorry."

I saw tears come to both parents' eyes as Cheryl sighed. "It's in God's hands now John, but look who's here to visit you! You remember Sam Reeve's little girl Louanne? Well this is her all growed up and in love with our son."

My mouth dropped open, unable to believe what she had just said. "Cheryl! I think you're jumping to conclusions. Travis and I barely know each other.."

Cheryl began to massage John's neck as he gave me the once over and began to write on his pad again. "Nonsense girl!" Exclaimed Cheryl.

"I know my son and my son is in love." She looked at what John had written. "John says he remembers you when you were little. Asks if you ever finished that vet thing you were doing."

I shook my head. This was becoming too much for me. I felt like I walked into the twilight zone. "No, Cheryl. You know I took over the bar for my father."

"Too bad," she replied. "John's probably thinking that a vet in the family would be good for the ranch."

"Excuse me, I think I need some coffee. Would you like some? I'm going to the cafeteria." I needed a break. This woman was the most meddlesome person I had ever come across. I suddenly couldn't imagine having her for a mother-in-law. Where did that come from? I asked myself. I'm getting tired. I couldn't imagine how tired she must be.

Cheryl declined my offer of coffee so I headed to the cafeteria, thankfully on my own for a bit. Once there I got my coffee and found a seat. Travis had been in the operating room for over an hour now. Surely there would be some word soon. How could Cheryl be jumping so far ahead? Had Travis said something to her? If so, how could HE be jumping so far ahead. Yes, right now she couldn't imagine life without him. She knew that she was in love and yes she hardly knew him. What if he were as controlling as his mother? I made up my mind that if Travis survived this, we would slow it down and take time to get to know each other before Cheryl rushed us to the altar. Finishing my coffee, I headed back to the waiting room leaving Cheryl with her husband. Frankly, I wasn't sure what to say to the man other than I hope you're feeling better soon or gee, why didn't you say you were sorry before now? I was tired, confused and sick at heart for Travis. What if he came away from this unable to be a rancher, or a lawyer? What if he ended up in the room next to his father, communicating by notes unable to fully function? Already I knew enough of Travis to know that he would never be happy like that. After I'd been sitting there and watching the clock for about a half an hour, Cheryl sat down beside me.

"It's taking forever isn't it?" She spoke quietly. She looked sad, and older, in just a few minutes.

"Cheryl, you need to get some sleep. Why don't you ask the nurses to put a cot in John's room?"

She shook her head. "No. Not until I know Travis is going to be alright." She took my hand. "Louanne, I owe you an apology. John helped me to see that I was pushing you too hard. I really like you. I always have and with my own daughters acting the way they have, well—I got to hoping having a girl I liked around the place would be real nice, but Travis has to make up his own mind and I guess he will on this too. I am sorry."

I squeezed her hand, grateful for her words. "Thank you Cheryl. You know, even if things don't work out for Travis and I, you are always welcome to visit me at the bar, always. I think Travis is a lucky man to have a mother who cares as much as you do."

"I want to go to the Chapel and say a prayer. Will you come with me? She asked.

I nodded, tears welling in my eyes, and hand in hand we walked towards the Chapel. Once inside we both approached the altar and knelt one on each side, to have some privacy in our thoughts and prayers.

Clasping my hands together, I bowed my head, as I didn't remember doing since my mother's funeral. "Dear God, please watch over

Travis and his family and be with them now in their hour of need. Be with Travis, Lord, make him strong and help him fight to come back to us." Tears were hot and salty on my lips as I prayed, "Please Lord hear my prayers", my heart cried "I'm so afraid." I rose and lit a candle for him. I could hear Cheryl sobbing through her prayer, her resolve finally beginning to crack. I went to her side and helped her stand.

She looked at me ."He'll be all right now. I know he will be."

Behind us, someone cleared their throat and we turned to see a nurse standing there with John Lester in a wheelchair. "He saw you both go by his room and he figured you were headed here. He insisted, rather vigorously, to be brought here too."

Tears welled up in Cheryl's eyes to see her husband of 33 years struggle to wheel his chair to where she stood and point at the notepad in his lap. She picked it up and read it out loud. "Time to pray for forgiveness and the life of my son." She burst into tears and threw her arms around her husband. "I never stopped believing in you John Lester, I never stopped believing." she sobbed. Then regaining her composure, she stood and took the handles of the wheelchair and wheeled John toward the altar.

    I stood in awe for a moment at the scene of love I had just witnessed. How wonderful to share grief and joy with someone you love. Someone that you're comfortable with just being who you are. Someone who loves you when you're at your very worst. My mother and father had that and it was now obvious that in their own way, Cheryl and John Lester had that. My heart whispered that maybe if I gave it time, Travis Lester could be the love I was looking for. "Maybe" whispered my heart "just maybe. Please Lord let him live!" I took a seat at the back of the chapel, giving Cheryl and John some privacy. I was saying my millionth prayer, it seemed, when the door opened and the Doctor treating Travis walked in.

Together, we walked to the altar where Cheryl and John waited. The doctor smiled. "He's going to make it. He'll be with us a while. Unfortunately, there was a lot of tendon damage. He'll need to do some physical therapy to get the strength back in his hands and his legs, but his injuries aren't permanent. "He's very lucky."

"Thank God!" said Cheryl, voicing all of our feelings. "Thank you Doc! I'll see to it that a certain bear rug comes your way by God!"

The doctor laughed. "That won't be necessary Mrs. Lester. Just tell Travis he owes me a steak dinner when he's up to it." He went on to inform us that we may as well go to a hotel and get some sleep because Travis wouldn't be up for company until morning.

All of our eyes gleamed as we walked with John back to his room. Once there, he wrote one more labored note to Cheryl. The wear of the day was beginning to show. It read, "I must see Travis as soon as possible."

Cheryl hesitated. I knew what she was thinking. John might want to see Travis, but Travis might not want to see his father. She patted his shoulder as the nurse helped him back into bed. " As soon as you can John, you'll see him, I promise."

At the hotel, Cheryl, Mike and I ate a quiet dinner. Happy, but too tired for much conversation. In my room I laid awake for a while thinking how important it was to tell people when you have a chance and each time you had a chance, how very much they mean to you. What a waste of all the years of bitter silence between father and son. How precious time is. I finally drifted off to sleep with Travis's aqua blue eyes on my mind.

The next morning I realized that all I had to wear were the same clothes from yesterday. I showered and asked Cheryl if I could borrow the limo and the driver for a quick shopping trip. She smiled and quickly said yes, realizing that as anxious as I was to see Travis I wanted to look my best for him. At a nearby mall I bought some new jeans and a jean shirt cut to fit a lady. I wasted no time looking for anything else because I wanted to get back to the hospital as quickly as I could. I bought a huge bunch of carnations for Travis and a little bear holding a heart. I laughed, thinking that the bear looked nothing like a grizzly but more like the kind of bear I wished Travis had encountered.

At the hospital, Cheryl and Mike were already in Travis's room when I arrived..

Travis was sitting up, pale, but smiling. His smile widened when our eyes met. "Louanne! Mom was just teasing me that I imagined you being here yesterday." I handed him the flowers and the bear but he barely noticed. His eyes locked on mine. "But I knew I couldn't have imagined that kiss!" He pulled me down and kissed my cheek, whispering in my ear. "You just wait till I'm outta here!"

I blushed. "Travis! Oh Travis, I'm so glad you're okay." I was going to continue but as I straightened up I saw he wasn't looking at me anymore but at the doorway where his father was sitting in his wheelchair.

"What's he doing here!" he snarled, "I don't want anything to do with him!"

Cheryl spoke up. "Travis Jordan Lester! You will show some respect to your father!" Then her voice softened and she patted Travis's arm. "It's time you and he talked, Travis-- please."

Travis brushed her hand away. "Get out! All of you except Louanne. Leave now!"

"Travis-" Cheryl started.

Travis's blue eyes turned to ice. "Get out! I don't want him here or anyone who sides with him!"

I took Cheryl outside the room and spoke to her and John. "Leave him with Mike for a minute. He'll calm down and then I'll try to make him see."

I walked back in and heard Mike saying, "Travis, your father is an old man. It's time to settle this before it's too late."

Travis was frowning, his eyes focused on the glorious colors of leaves on the trees outside the window. I walked around the bed and took his hand. Mike shook his head, realizing he wasn't going to get through to him and left.

I raised his hand to my lips and kissed his raw knuckles. "Travis, your father prayed with us in the chapel last night for your life. It's time to heal your body and both of your hearts. Please talk to him."

Just then I saw tears welling in his eyes as his father painfully wheeled his chair up to the bedside. His father reached out his hand and grasped Travis's hand. Travis winced and tears rolled down his cheeks. He didn't look at his father but he didn't pull away. The unbearable silence was broken finally as John Lester struggled to form words.

Tears flowed freely down his face with emotion and effort until, with painful slowness, he said " Love–you–son." And squeezed his son's hand. Travis turned to look in his father's eyes for the first time in ten years. I released his hand and sighed with happiness as he closed it over his father's. I left them to let the healing begin.

All that seems like years ago now. With a long painful rehabilitation, both father and son got well. They worked as a team. Travis and I spent long hours together and in the fall of the following year, surrounded by tumbling aspen leaves and glorious Indian summer colors, John Lester walked me down the aisle to meet his son. We had chosen autumn to wed because to us, it symbolized the end of our lonely lives. I'm writing this from the log home Travis built for us on a lake higher in the mountains. Travis sold his partner his share of the law practice and Stu and Sally bought my bar. The only things remaining from those days are Travis' framed law degree, all my pictures of my mother and father that had hung behind the bar, and the 'Louannes' neon sign that Travis had insisted we hang in our den--- along with a certain bear rug.

As I watch my handsome husband cradling his newborn son, Travis John Lester Jr. on our porch, I finally understand the love my parents had and I'm grateful to God for their example and the chance to see the world through my son's aqua blue eyes.

The End